little Miss Tiny

by Roger Hargreaves

WORLD INTERNATIONAL

Little Miss Tiny was extremely small.

Not very tall at all!

She was so very tiny she didn't live in a house.

Do you know where she lived?

In a mousehole, in the dining room of
Home Farm.

She had made the mousehole quite comfortable really, and luckily there weren't any mice because the farm cat had chased them all away.

The trouble was, because she was so tiny, nobody knew she lived there.

Nobody had noticed her.

Not even the farmer and his wife.

So, there she lived.

All alone.

With nobody to talk to.

She was very lonely.

And sad.

Oh dear!

One day she was feeling so lonely she decided to be very brave and go for a walk.

Out of her mousehole she came.

She crept across the dining room and went through the crack in the door and into the hall.

To little Miss Tiny the hall looked as big as a field, and she scuttled across it to the back door of the farm.

Luckily for her the letterbox was at the bottom of the door and she squeezed herself through it and onto the doorstep.

It was all very exciting!

There before her was the farmyard.

She went exploring.

She came to a door with a gap at the bottom, and ducked in underneath.

There, inside, was a pig.

A large pig!

And, if you're as small as little Miss Tiny, a large pig looks very large indeed.

Miss Tiny looked at the pig.

The pig looked at Miss Tiny.

"Oink," he grunted, and moved closer to inspect this little person who had entered his sty.

"Oh my goodness me," squeaked little Miss Tiny in alarm, and shot out of the pigsty as fast as ever her little legs would carry her.

Which wasn't very fast because her legs were so very little!

She ran right around to the back of the pigsty before she stopped.

She leaned against the wall and put her hands over her eyes, and tried to get her breath back.

Suddenly, she heard a noise.

A very close noise.

A sort of breathing noise.

Very close indeed!

Oh!

She hardly dared take her hands away from her eyes, but when she did she wished she hadn't.

What do you think it was, there, right in front of her, looking at her with green eyes?

Ginger!

The farm cat!!

Poor little Miss Tiny.

Ginger grinned, showing his teeth.

"HELP!" shrieked Miss Tiny at the top of her voice.

"Oh somebody please HELP!"

The trouble was, the top of little Miss Tiny's voice was not a very loud place.

Ginger grinned another grin.

Every day Mr Strong went to Home Farm to buy some eggs.

He liked eggs.

Lots of them.

That day he was walking home across the farmyard when he heard a very tiny squeak.

He stopped.

There it was again.

Round the corner.

He looked round the corner and saw Ginger and the poor trapped little Miss Tiny.

"SHOO!" said Mr Strong to Ginger, and picked up little Miss Tiny.

Very gently.

"Hello," he said. "Who are you?"

"I'm... I'm... I'm... Miss Tiny."

"You are, aren't you?" smiled Mr Strong.

"Well, if I was as tiny as you, I wouldn't go wandering around large farmyards!"

"But..." said Miss Tiny, and told Mr Strong about how she was so lonely she had to come out to find somebody to talk to.

"Oh dear," said Mr Strong. "Well now, let's see if we can't find you some friends to talk to."

And now, every week, Mr Strong collects little Miss Tiny and takes her off to see her friends.

Three weeks ago he took her to see Mr Funny, who told her so many jokes she just couldn't stop laughing all day.

Two weeks ago he took her to see Mr Greedy.

He told her his recipe for his favourite meal.

"But that's much much too much for tiny little me," she laughed.

Mr Greedy grinned.

"For you," he said, "divide by a hundred!"

Last week Mr Strong took her to see Mr Silly.

And Mr Silly showed her how to stand on your head.

"That's very silly", giggled little Miss Tiny.

"Thank you", replied Mr Silly, modestly.

And guess who she met this week?

Somebody who's become a special little friend.

"I never thought I'd ever meet anybody smaller than myself," laughed Mr Small.

Little Miss Tiny looked up at him, and smiled.

"You wait till I grow up," she said.

Mr Men and Little Miss Library Presentation Boxes

In response to the many thousands of requests for the above, we are delighted to advise that these are now available direct from ourselves, for only **£4.99** (inc VAT) plus 50p p&p.
The full colour boxes accommodate each complete library. They have an integral carrying handle as well as a neat stay closed fastener.
Please do not send cash in the post. Cheques should be made payable to **World International Ltd. for the sum of £5.49** (inc p&p) per box.

Please note books are not included.

Please return this page with your cheque, stating below which presentation box you would like, to:-
Mr Men Office, World International
PO Box 7, Manchester, M19 2HD

Your name:_____

Address: _____

_____

_____Postcode: _____

Name of Parent/Guardian (please print):_____

Signature:_____

I enclose a cheque for £_____ made payable to World International Ltd.,

Please send me a Mr Men Presentation Box ☐

Little Miss Presentation Box ☐   (please tick or write in quantity) and allow 28 days for delivery

Thank you

Offer applies to UK, Eire & Channel Isles only

MORE SPECIAL OFFERS
FOR MR MEN AND LITTLE MISS READERS

In every Mr Men and Little Miss book like this one, and now in the Mr Men sticker and activity books, you will find a special token. Collect six tokens and we will send you a gift of your choice
Choose either a Mr Men or Little Miss poster, **or** a Mr Men or Little Miss **double sided** full colour bedroom door hanger.

Return this page **with six tokens per gift required** to:

Marketing Dept., MM / LM, World International Ltd., PO Box 7, Manchester, M19 2HD

Your name:_____ Age: _____

Address: _____

_____

_____Postcode: _____

Parent / Guardian Name (Please Print)_____

Please tape a 20p coin to your request to cover part post and package cost

I enclose <u>six</u> tokens per gift, and 20p please send me:-

Posters:- Mr Men Poster ☐ Little Miss Poster ☐

Door Hangers - Mr Nosey / Muddle ☐ Mr Greedy / Lazy ☐

Mr Tickle / Grumpy ☐ Mr Slow / Busy ☐

Mr Messy / Quiet ☐ Mr Perfect / Forgetful ☐

L Miss Fun / Late ☐ L Miss Helpful / Tidy ☐

L Miss Busy / Brainy ☐ L Miss Star / Fun ☐

20p

Stick 20p here please

Please Tick Appropriate Box ☐

We may occasionally wish to advise you of other Mr Men gifts.
If you would rather we didn't please tick this box

|← 100 mm →|

ENTRANCE FEE
3 SAUSAGES

250 mm

MR.GREEDY

Collect six of these tokens
You will find one inside every
Mr Men and Little Miss book
which has this special offer.

1
TOKEN

Offer open to residents of UK, Channel Isles and Ireland only